The Littles
and their Friends

HOUSE
TREE
BROOK
TRASH
GROUND
TINIES

The Littles and their Friends

A facsimile reproduction of
pages from a tiny person's
book enlarged six times.

by WILLIAM T. LITTLE with help from JOHN PETERSON

SCHOLASTIC INC.
New York Toronto London Auckland Sydney

To all tiny people

ISBN 0-590-31394-0

12 11 10 9 8 7 6 5 9/9 0 1 2/0

Printed in the U.S.A. 08

How I discovered the Littles

Before I began writing books about the Littles — before I discovered the Littles — I made a living doing odd jobs.

One day my neighbor, George W. Bigg, asked me to replace a patch of dirty wallpaper in his living room. I was pulling off the old wallpaper near the ceiling when I noticed something strange: there were pinholes in the paper.

Then I found a round hole under the pinholes. A cork was stuck in the hole. I pulled the cork out and looked through the hole. I was amazed. There was a tiny living room inside the wall!

I yelled for Mr. Bigg to come. Then I remembered that the Biggs weren't home.

I began to examine the tiny room. Much of the small furniture was made from things that could have been found around the Biggs' house. A vitamin bottle was an end-table; a thimble was used as a waste basket; a tuna fish can was a hassock. The pictures on the wall were postage stamps.

There was a pocket watch over the mantlepiece — and it was ticking! Someone must have wound it that very day. A tiny book lay open on the tuna fish hassock. I picked up the book with a pair of tweezers.

I used Mr. Bigg's magnifying glass to look at the book. The title was: THE TINY PEOPLE. It was written by a Mr. William T. Little.

The book told about the adventures of Mr. Little's family. The Littles were a tiny people. They were less than six inches tall! They looked just like big people except that they had tails.

Many of these tiny people live in houses. Not all tiny people are House Tinies however. Tree Tinies live in trees in the woods. Ground Tinies live underground among tree roots. Brook Tinies live in caves near the brook. Trash Tinies live under the town dump. The book had pictures (drawn by Mr. Little) and descriptions of how the tiny people lived, what they ate, how they traveled — everything about them.

I learned that all tiny people keep a close watch on us. Their greatest fear

is that big people will discover that tiny people are living among them.

Some "Tinies" think that big people would kill them like mice. Others believe they would be put in circus sideshows like freaks. Some think that big people might experiment on them.

You can imagine how I felt. I had just made one of the greatest discoveries in history. I wanted to tell everyone. But I didn't want to do anything to change the Littles' wonderful way of life.

Luckily the Littles weren't at home when I found out their secret. I put the book back on the hassock. I replaced the cork and pasted up the new wallpaper. Then I put pinholes in the right place.

Before I did that, I made photocopies of everything in Mr. Little's book. You are about to see some pages that I copied. What I found most interesting were the drawings that showed how the different Tinies lived. These pages have been enlarged six times. Now you can discover for yourself the world of these remarkable people without using a magnifying glass.

John Peterson

DR. DAN ZIGGER'S HOUSE
AUNT LILY LIVES HERE
GROUND TINIES
WHIT SNIPPET'S RABBIT HOLE
SHORTS
STUBBY SPECK'S OAK TREE
LITTLES
TREE TINIES
Path through the woods
The Brook
Path
SMALLS
CRUMS
Henry Bigg's toy Sailboat
The Pond
foot bridge
DAM
BUTTONS
(where Dinky and Della were married)

OUR LAND–
THE BIG VALLEY
Showing where the Tiny People live
Note: House Tinies live in houses
marked with
TRASH TINIES
TRASH CITY
UNDER TOWN
DUMP
(Mayor Clutter lives in an
orange crate)
BROOK TINIES
LIMESTONE CAVES
LONG EDDY BURNS'S CAVE
THE DARK WOODS
S
W
E
N
The Brook
Grandpa's
tree stump
house
The Island
The
River
Unknown
Territory

THE LITTLES

Tom is ten years old (almost eleven). He tamed Hildy, the Biggs' cat.

Uncle Nick is a retired major from the army of the Trash Tinies.

Lucy is eight years old. Mostly she is brave, but she is afraid of mice.

Uncle Pete was a crack shot during the Mouse Invasion of '35.

Grandpa is an explorer and inventor. He discovered the Brook Tinies.

Granny Little makes everyone's clothes. She makes them from things around the Biggs' house.

Baby Betsy

Cousin Dinky and Della are adventurers. They deliver the mail to all the tiny people.

Mr. Little, on the roof of the Biggs' house waiting for the mail to drop in the chimney net.

Aunt Lily learned how to be a nurse by watching a big doctor.

Mrs. Little (Wilma) gets all the family's food from the Biggs' leftovers.

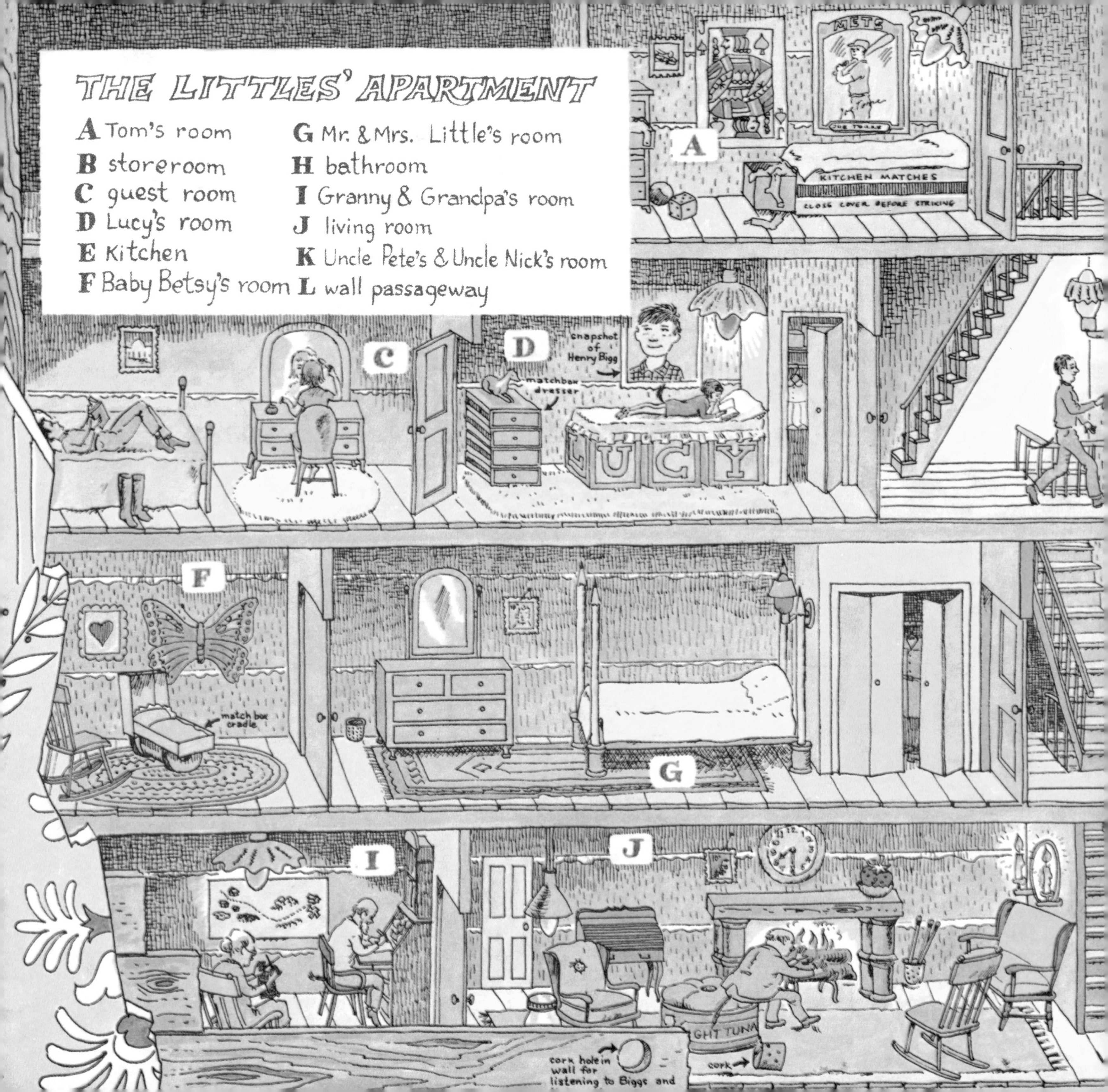
THE LITTLES' APARTMENT
A Tom's room
B storeroom
C guest room
D Lucy's room
E Kitchen
F Baby Betsy's room
G Mr. & Mrs. Little's room
H bathroom
I Granny & Grandpa's room
J living room
K Uncle Pete's & Uncle Nick's room
L wall passageway
METS
A
KITCHEN MATCHES
CLOSE COVER BEFORE STRIKING
C
D
snapshot of Henry Bigg
matchbox dresser
LUCY
F
match box cradle
G
I
J
GHT TUNA
cork
cork hole in wall for listening to Biggs and

B
K
UNITED STATES OF AMERICA
ONE DOLLAR
H
L
shell sink
ONION FLAKES
CROWN PRINCE
SARDINES
Tomato
SOUP
tin-can elevator
E
dried food
imitation mayonnaise
Black Pepper
GROUND
Cloves
L

bottle-bottom window
moss rug
Old Skunk

plastic dixie-cup sink
pure rain water from tree-top reservoir
THE TREE TINIES
Mr. and Mrs. Stubby Speck and their two daughters live in a giant oak tree in the woods near the Biggs' house. Their eight snug rooms are whittled out of the tree. Sunlight streams through the colored bottle-bottom windows. A long oak table and chairs grow right out of the floor. They are part of the living tree. There are other Tree Tinies living nearby.

water for shower and toilet piped in from nearby spring
Mr. Snippet with his pet deer mouse
tin-can top mirror
To store room
mole-skin rug (Very soft)

entrance
rabbit burrow
tunnel to Snippets' home from rabbit burrow.
THE GROUND TINIES
Mr. and Mrs. Whit Snippet and their two sons live under a maple tree southeast of us. We discovered them while searching for our lost Aunt Lily. There are many Ground Tinies in the woods. They are very shy and live in rabbit burrows. Their homes begin where the rabbit burrows end. Much of their furniture is made by bending the live tree roots.
stone sink
cellar of rabbit burrow
deer mouse hole

THE TRASH TINIES
Mayor Clutter and his family live in Trash City, a secret place underneath the town dump. The tiny people are always guarding against an attack from their enemies – mice! Major Nick Little is their hero; he organized the Army of the Trash Tinies. Everyone lives comfortably because big people throw away so many useful things.
COMMUNITY YOUTH CENTER
ASHS

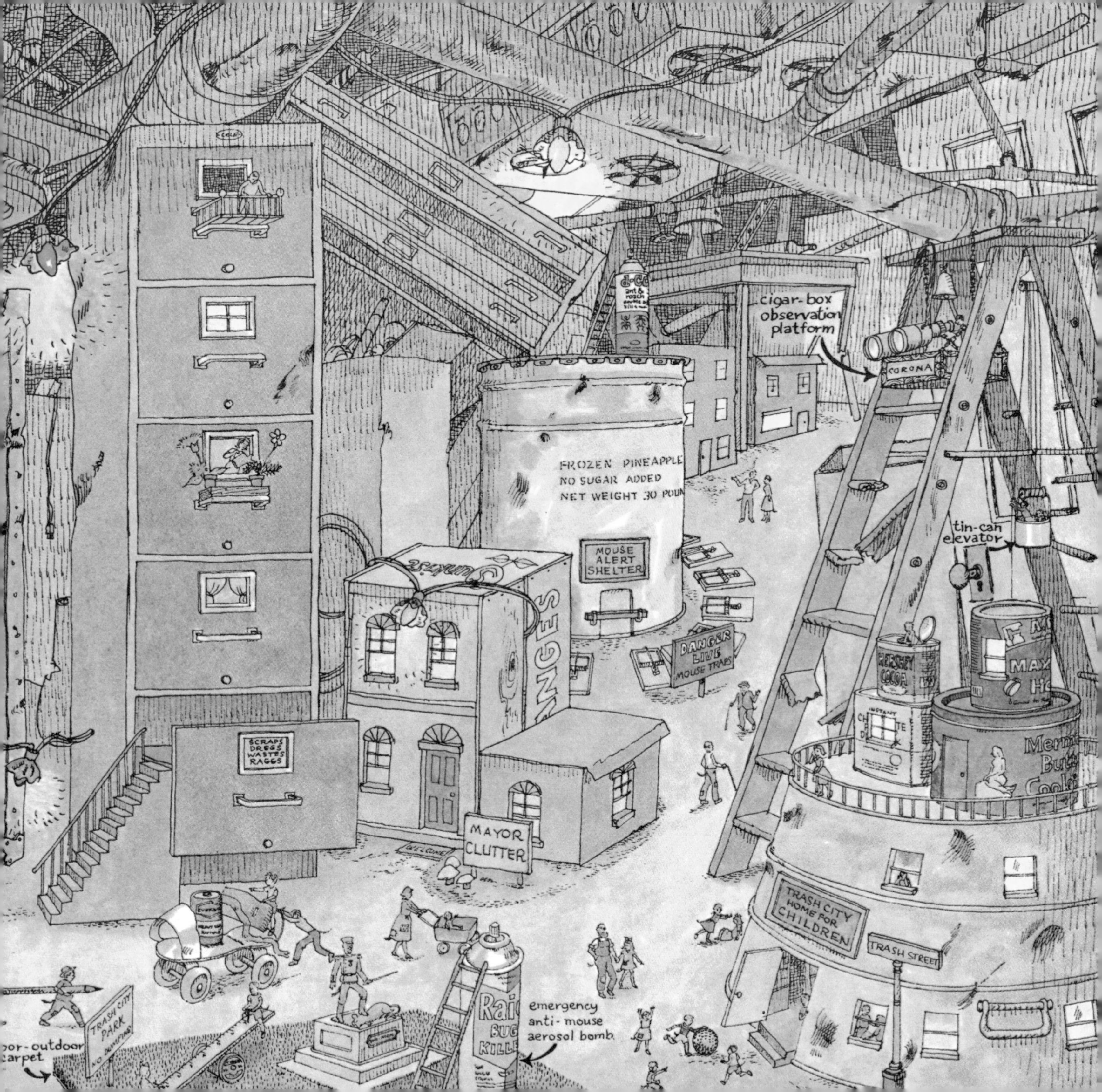

cigar-box observation platform
CORONA
FROZEN PINEAPPLE
NO SUGAR ADDED
MOUSE ALERT SHELTER
tin-can elevator
DANGER LIVE MOUSE TRAPS
HERSHEY COCOA
SCRAPS DREGS WASTES RAGGS
MAYOR CLUTTER
WELCOME
TRASH CITY HOME FOR CHILDREN
TRASH STREET
emergency anti-mouse aerosol bomb.
TRASH CITY PARK NO DUMPING

THE BROOK TINIES
Mr. and Mrs. "Long Eddy" Burns and their twenty children live in a cave near the brook. Many Brook Tiny families live in this part of the Dark Woods. They love the water, and spend much time swimming, diving, and fishing. We visited them in our toy boat, The Discoverer, while searching for Grandpa Little who was lost on an exploring trip.

A note from the author

I have written twelve books about the Littles and I hope to write more. I never could have written them without the help of Mr. Little's book. It is full of information about the way tiny people live.

Much of what I wrote I had to make up; especially when it had to do with conversations among tiny people. Mr. Little's book tells all about the personalities of his family and friends. This helped me to imagine what everyone said and did.

The books I wrote were illustrated by my friend Roberta Carter Clark. We are the only people in the world who know about the Big Valley and where the tiny people live. We have sworn an oath to tell no one. The tiny people will continue to live among us secretly as they have for hundreds of years.

J.P.

HOUSE
TREE
BROOK
TRASH
GROUND
TINIES